The Alien on the 99th Floor

Written by Jenny Nimmo

Illustrated by Julian Mosedal

1 The 99th floor

The day Fred Hopkin met an alien began really badly.
Fred's mother wanted some new shoes.

"Come on," she said to Fred. "We're going shopping!"

"I hate shopping," Fred said.

He'd just coloured his face with face paint. It made his baby sister, Sophie, laugh, but Mrs Hopkin didn't think it was funny. There was no time to wash Fred's face and they had to run to catch the bus.

The shopping centre was very crowded. Sophie sat in her pushchair, biting her red ball. It played "Pop goes the weasel", when she rattled it.

"Can we go to the toy shop?" asked Fred.

"Toys!" yelled Sophie.

"Well ..." Mrs Hopkin looked in the toy shop. The place was crammed with children. They were grabbing and pushing and crawling and jumping and shouting.

"I can't take Sophie in there!" Mrs Hopkin cried.

"Please," begged Fred. He'd just seen a new computer game. It was called "The Alien on the 99th Floor". On the front there was a picture of a giant silver bubble and the words: "He can see you, but you can't see him!"

But Mrs Hopkin was dragging them away to the lift.

"Can I have that game?" asked Fred. "Can I ..."

"No," said his mother. "Come on, Fred, the shoe shop's on the next floor."

The lift arrived, the doors slid open and everyone pushed in. A man trod on Fred's foot, and a woman put her bag on his head.

The shoe shop was boring, so Fred tried on
a sparkly cap.

"Yeah! Yeah! Yeah!" yelled Sophie.

"Fred, take it off!" said his mother.

Then Sophie threw her ball across the floor.
Fred crawled over to get it, pretending to be a dog.

"Pop goes the weasel!" sang the ball.

A woman trying on shoes nearly tripped over Fred.
"What's that boy doing here?" she shrieked.

Mrs Hopkin said sorry and dragged Fred and the pushchair away.

"Can we go to ..." Fred began.

"I need a cup of tea!" said his mother.

The lift wasn't as full this time. A man asked, "Which floor?"

"Ninety-nine," Fred said grimly.

Mrs Hopkin laughed and said, "We want the café on the top floor!"

At the top floor, everyone got out.
Everyone, except Fred.

"Come on, Fred," called
Mrs Hopkin.

Fred didn't move.
The doors clanged shut
and he was alone.
And then something
very weird happened.
The lights went out
and the lift began
to move. Faster and
faster and faster.
Up and up and up!

9

2 "Are you an alien?"

Fred's head began to spin. Where was the lift going now?

There was a clunking noise and it stopped.

Very slowly, the doors opened. Fred put his foot out. The ground was hard and sort of frosty. He must be on the roof of the shops, but very high up.
There were no lights and no sounds, only the wind.

Fred wasn't sure about leaving the lift. What if it went away without him? He stepped out and peered around.

"Oh!" gasped Fred, for there was the giant silver bubble that he'd seen on the computer game.

He felt its silky, rubbery surface. Was it really a spaceship?

There was a window and Fred peeped inside.

A small person in a glittery suit was sitting on the floor. Lights were blinking and buttons buzzing all around him. But the little person took no notice. He was crying.

"Hey!" Fred banged on the window.

The stranger looked up and Fred was amazed to see a patterned face, just like his.

Then a door opened into the bubble. Fred went
inside and the door zipped shut behind him.
"Hi!" he said, "I'm Fred!"

The stranger looked pleased. He pointed at himself
with a long spiky finger and made a sound like an
owl's hoot. "Ooo!"

"Ooo," said Fred, in a low voice. "Are you ... are you
an *alien?*"

The stranger nodded.

"You are! So what's the problem?"

Ooo pointed to a small hole in the wall of
the spaceship. Fred put his hand over the hole,
and the bubble made a strange humming sound.

"Weeee!" cried the alien, jumping for joy.

Fred took his hand away and the humming
died down.

"Awwwww!" the alien moaned.

"I can't keep my hand there forever," Fred told him, and he gazed around for something to push into the hole. There was nothing except a fluffy yellow toy on a string. It had six legs and lots of eyes, but it was too small to fill the hole.

Fred felt in his pockets and pulled out Sophie's red ball. "Pop goes the weasel!" it sang.

"Eeee!" cried Ooo, clapping his hands.

"OK," said Fred, "let's try it."

He pushed it into the hole. It fitted perfectly.

The bubble started to hum, louder and louder.
Then it moved.

"Wait!" Fred shouted.

Now they were spinning in circles. Faster and
faster and faster.

"STOP!" yelled Fred.

3 "He can see you, but you can't see him!"

Ooo stared at Fred.

"I'm going to be sick," yelled Fred.

The alien pressed a button and the space bubble stopped spinning. Ooo put his head on one side. He seemed to be saying he was sorry.

Fred smiled. "That's better. But I can't come with you now," he said. "I've got to get back to Mum. She'll be wondering where I am."

Ooo nodded wisely. He took the yellow toy and put it into Fred's hand.

"Wow!" said Fred. "For me?"

Ooo grinned from ear to ear. "Wow!" he repeated, as though Fred had guessed the toy's name.
Then he pointed to Sophie's ball. "Pop goes!" he said.

"OK, I'll swap it for the ball," Fred agreed.
"Thanks, Ooo!"

Then Fred remembered the words on the computer game. There was something he had to ask. "You *are* the alien on the 99th floor, aren't you? So why aren't you invisible? On the computer game it says: 'He can see you, but you can't see him.'"

Ooo smiled and, out of his pocket, he took a sparkly cap. He pulled it over his head.

Very slowly, Ooo began to disappear, until all Fred could see was a little shining cloud like the steam from a kettle.

"I wish I could do that!" cried Fred.

Then the cloud floated over to him and an invisible finger touched his arm. It felt tingly. Then Fred began to vanish, too. First his arms, his body, his legs and last of all, his feet.

It was weird, not seeing your body and yet knowing it was there. Fred started thinking. There were so many things an invisible boy could do.

He said to the cloud, "There's somewhere I want to go before I go back to Mum and Sophie. It's called a toy shop. Do you want to come?"

The cloud whizzed around excitedly.

"Let's go, then," said Fred.

The door slid open and they sailed out into the cold air towards the lift.

4 "Stop that!"

The lift slid down, down, down. The doors didn't open until the lift clunked to a standstill beside the toy shop.

Fred and Ooo went into the shop. Ooo grabbed a pair of roller blades and put them on. Fred picked up another pair, and then they were off.

"Hey!" called the manager.

Fred and Ooo zoomed behind a group of children.

"Stop that!" yelled the manager.

"It isn't us," said the children, as two pairs of roller blades whizzed past.

Then everyone began to clap, while the manager chased after them shouting, "Who's doing this?"

"It must be the alien from the 99th floor," laughed a boy.

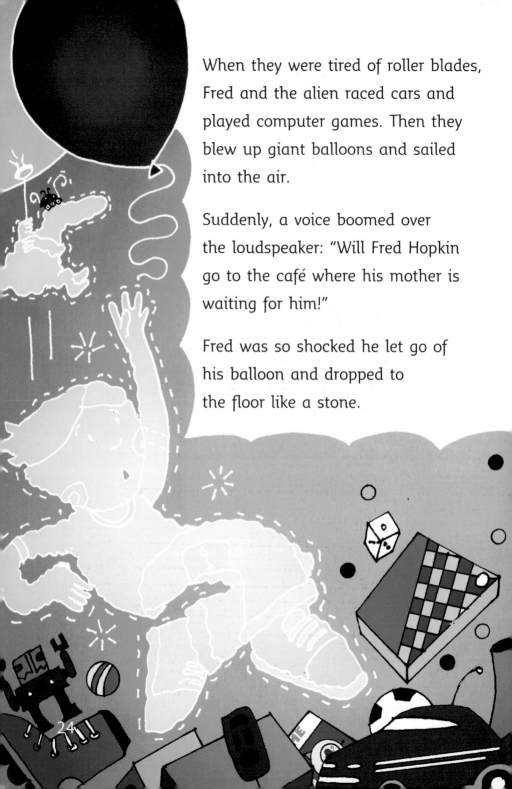

When they were tired of roller blades, Fred and the alien raced cars and played computer games. Then they blew up giant balloons and sailed into the air.

Suddenly, a voice boomed over the loudspeaker: "Will Fred Hopkin go to the café where his mother is waiting for him!"

Fred was so shocked he let go of his balloon and dropped to the floor like a stone.

5 "Where have you been?"

Fred raced for the lift. A small cloud whizzed in behind him just as the doors were closing.

In the empty lift, someone said, "Hm!" in a cross voice.

"Sorry, Ooo," said Fred. "I didn't mean to leave you behind. It's my mum. She's looking for me."

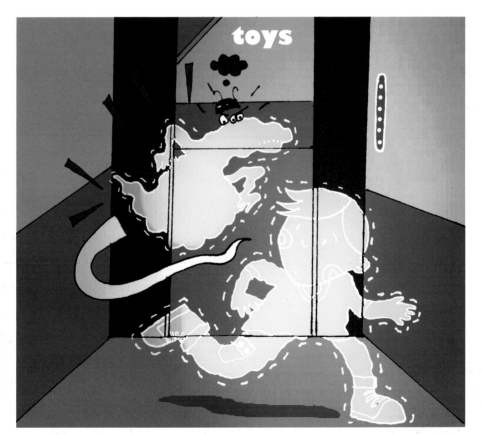

There was a tug on his invisible tee shirt.

"Oh, no!" cried Fred. "Mum won't be able to see me!"

A tingly finger touched Fred's arm.

Fred felt a weird, buzzing feeling and slowly he got himself back: feet, legs, body and all.

As the doors slid open again, Fred was sure the alien was smiling at him.

"Bye, Ooo!" Fred called, smiling back at his invisible friend. "Got to go!"

Fred ran to the café and there was Mum, looking
very upset.

"Fred!" she cried, hugging him tightly. "Where *have*
you been?"

Then Sophie started yelling: "Pop! Pop! Pop!"

27

Fred couldn't tell them where the red ball had gone.
But he had a present for Sophie. Out of his pocket
he pulled the little yellow toy with six legs and lots
of eyes.

"Wow!" cried Sophie.

"How did you guess its name?" asked Fred.

As they left the shopping centre, Fred thought about Ooo sailing through the universe in a silver bubble that sang, "Pop goes the weasel". Would he ever see the little alien again?

"Oh, no!" Mrs Hopkin cried. "I forgot the shoes!"

"Let's come here again next Saturday," Fred suggested.

His mum stared at him. "But you hate shopping!"

"Not always," said Fred.

Paint your face, and join in the game.

Do you dare

Rocket up to the 99th floor!

ZOOM

up to the 99th floor

Meet the friendly alien with the painted face.

to play with

the Alien?

Explore the giant silver spaceship.

:paw: Ideas for guided reading :paw:

Learning objectives: infer characters' feelings; use syntax, context and word structure to build their store of vocabulary as they read for meaning; use some drama strategies to explore stories or issues

Curriculum links: Art and Design: Viewpoints; Citizenship: Choices

Interest words: alien, coloured, shrieked, 99, clanged, weird, frosty, peered, rubbery, glittery, patterned, invisible

Resources: magazine adverts for computer games, internet sites for computer games

Getting started

This book can be read over two or more guided reading sessions.

- Ask children to describe what an alien is, and to recount any stories with aliens that they already know.

- Read the title and blurb together. Discuss how the children would feel and what they would do if they found an alien who needed their help.

Reading and responding

- Model reading aloud pp2–3, using expression to reflect meaning making.

- Create a freeze frame of the point in the story where Fred's mum sees Fred's face and says he has to go shopping. Ask children to suggest what each character is thinking at that point *(thought tracking)*.

- Ask children to read pp4–9 individually, making a note of how Fred is feeling during the chapter. Model how to infer his feelings from what is written, e.g. *he is probably bored so he paints his face!*

- Reread p9 aloud to the children. Ask them to close their eyes and imagine that they are Fred in the lift. Discuss what Fred might be thinking and what he might be saying to himself.